This Little Tiger book belongs to:

_____

_____

_____

For Daniel
~J.S.

For Chris and Sal's new baby
~J.C.

LITTLE TIGER PRESS
An imprint of Magi Publications
1 The Coda Centre, 189 Munster Road
London SW6 6AW
www.littletigerpress.com
First published in Great Britain 2002
by Little Tiger Press, London
This edition published 2010
Text copyright © 2002 Julie Sykes
Illustrations copyright © 2002 Jane Chapman
Julie Sykes and Jane Chapman have asserted their
rights to be identified as the author and illustrator of this work
under the Copyright, Designs and Patents Act, 1988
All rights reserved
ISBN 978-1-84895-187-7
Printed in China
2 4 6 8 10 9 7 5 3 1

DORA'S CHICKS

by Julie Sykes   Illustrated by Jane Chapman

LITTLE TIGER PRESS

One morning, Dora opened her eyes.

Her six fluffy chicks were beginning to stir.

"My chicks will be hungry," clucked Dora.

"I'd better go and look for their breakfast."

Dora hopped out of the henhouse
and into the yard. She was only gone
for a minute, but when she came back,
the henhouse was empty!
"Where are my six chicks?" cried Dora.

Quickly, Dora ran back into the barnyard
and over to the pigpen.
"Hello, Penny," she called. "I've lost my
chicks. Have you seen them?"
"Sorry, Dora, I'm feeding my piglets,"
oinked Penny. "I haven't noticed
where your chicks have gone."

Dora watched the piglets
rushing toward their mother.
But who was that following them?

It was one of her chicks! "Stop!" she clucked. "Chicks don't nurse for their food."

Dora hopped after her chick and rescued it before it got trampled. "One chick safe," said Dora, feeling a little happier. "But that leaves five to find."

Dora and her one chick went down to the pond.
Debbie Duck was there, getting her ducklings
into line.
"Hello, Debbie," called Dora. "I've lost some chicks.
Have you seen them?"
"I'm teaching my ducklings to fish for their food,"
quacked Debbie. "So I haven't seen where
your chicks have gone."

Dora watched the ducklings splash into the water. The last one couldn't keep up. Suddenly, Dora realized it wasn't a duckling at all!

It was another of her chicks!
"Wait!" cried Dora. "Chicks don't
fish for food. They can't swim!"

Dora chased after her chick, and stopped it from jumping into the water just in the nick of time.

"Two chicks safe," said Dora, feeling quite pleased. "But that leaves four to find."

Dora continued on her search. On the way past the
big barn she stopped to look inside. Honey Horse
was showing her foal how to eat hay.
"Hello, Honey," called Dora. "I've lost
some chicks. Have you seen them?"
"Sorry, Dora, but I've been so busy
with my foal, I haven't noticed
your chicks," neighed Honey.

Sadly, Dora hopped back
toward the door. But who
was that climbing those
bales of hay?

"*Two* of my chicks," cried Dora with relief. Quickly, she rescued them before they slipped and fell. "Chicks don't eat hay," said Dora, as she pushed her brood over to the door.

Back in the sunlight, Dora counted
her chicks.
"One, two, three, four. But I have six
chicks, so there are still two missing."

Dora searched everywhere for her last two chicks.
She searched in the yard, and she searched in the
orchard. She squeezed under the gate and . . .

saw Bobby Bird on the other side
of the road, pulling up worms to eat.
"Cheep, cheep, cheep," cried Dora's chicks,
feeling hungry. "We want breakfast!"

Dora was just about to turn back,
when she saw . . .

her fifth chick crossing the road
to reach Bobby and his worms.
"Don't move!" ordered Dora.
"You must *never* cross a road
without looking both ways
first. You might get hurt."

Bobby flew over to see
what all the fuss was about.
"Goodness, what a lot
of chicks," he exclaimed.
"Yes," said Dora. "But I
have six chicks, so one is
still missing."

Dora and her chicks hopped through
the upper field. They flapped across
the lower field.

They passed the cowshed and the doghouse. And all the time, Dora kept looking for her sixth chick.

The other five chicks were tired.
"We're hungry," they complained.
At last Dora knew she must take
the chicks home and feed them.

Sadly, she headed back to the henhouse.
The little chicks hurried after her.
"Cheep, cheep, cheep," they cried.
"Breakfast!"
Dora saw the grain scattered in the yard,
but she didn't feel hungry.
"Where is my sixth chick?" she clucked.

"Here I am!" chirped a tiny voice. Dora's sixth chick was already back in the yard, pecking for breakfast! Dora clucked with joy. At last all her chicks were home again.

"Excuse me, Dora, can you help me?
I need to find some moss for my nest."
It was Bobby Bird.
"We'll help you, Bobby," said Dora,
"as soon the chicks are finished
with breakfast!"

More fantastic reads from Little Tiger Press!

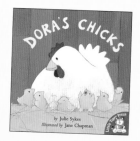

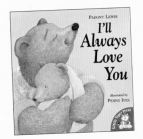

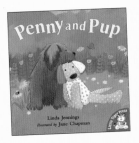

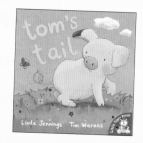

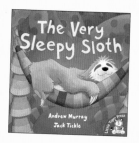

For information regarding any of the above titles or for our catalog, please contact us:
Little Tiger Press, 1 The Coda Centre, 189 Munster Road, London SW6 6AW, UK
Tel: +44 (0)20 7385 6333 • Fax: +44 (0)20 7385 7333 E-mail: info@littletiger.co.uk • www.littletigerpress.com